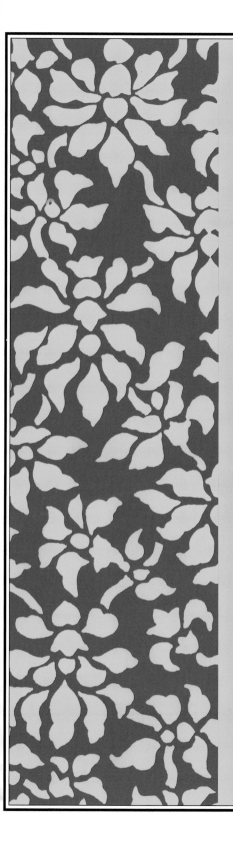

THE
TWO
BROTHERS

BY
MINFONG HO & SAPHAN ROS
ILLUSTRATED BY
JEAN & MOU-SIEN TSENG

LOTHROP, LEE & SHEPARD BOOKS
NEW YORK

AUTHOR'S NOTE

THE DIVERSITY OF CAMBODIA'S FOLKTALES reflects the country's long and rich history, dating back almost two thousand years to the 1st century A.D., when its royal courts adopted an alphabet and a legal code. From the 9th to the 13th centuries the Khmer empire extended far into the kingdoms of its neighbors, Thailand, Laos, and Vietnam. More recently, during the years of the Vietnam War, the superpowers of the United States and the Soviet Union used Cambodia as a pawn in their conflicts, resulting in terrible suffering for the Cambodians. The American bombing of Cambodia in the late '60s and early '70s was followed by the despotic genocidal rule of the Khmer Rouge from 1975–79. It is only recently that a fragile peace has been established.

Throughout their often tumultuous history, Cambodians have always handed down folktales, simple stories of rabbits and crocodiles, monks and kings—stories that reflect the richly woven texture of their society. Traditionally these folktales were told by grandparents to village children in the cool of evening. More elaborate presentations took the form of folk plays, known as *Yikay*. These were performed by small theatrical troupes that traveled from one village to another. Dancers pantomimed the action while a narrator sang the story to the accompaniment of drums or the two-stringed Khmer violin. Although the main story line remained traditional, the lively narrators and actors often improvised, adding details of local interest, much to the delight of their audience.

The story "The Two Brothers" reflects the rich texture of Cambodian life. In it we catch glimpses of a Buddhist monastery, the royal court, village life, and even of a mythological monster. Running through this complex tapestry is the age-old conflict between predestination and free will. Cambodians traditionally believe that one's fortune can be foretold by looking at astrological charts. Yet, as Buddhists, they also believe that each individual is free to choose how to live out his or her own life. In "The Two Brothers," this seeming contradiction is neatly reconciled: Kem followed the abbot's advice and helped make his own fortune come true, while his brother, Sem, did not, so that what had been foretold for him did not come about. Only when Sem finally actively followed the abbot's guidelines did his life change to fulfill his destiny.

Against the context of today's Cambodia, this story is especially poignant. The Cambodians have accepted the tragedy of their past with stoic fatalism, yet when given the chance to shape their own destinies, they have actively done so. During the United Nations–supervised elections of 1993, an impressive 90% of the electorate braved threats of violence to cast their ballots for a new government, a new chance at peace.

After so many terrible years of war and suffering, one can only hope that a lasting peace for Cambodia is written in the stars.

Minfong Ho
Ithaca, New York
1995

for Cambodian children and their friends, everywhere
—MH

I would like to dedicate this book to the memory of those of my family
who were killed during the Pol Pot reign.
This story is also for my children—Rithy, Chhorvy, Linda, and Duong—
from whom I was separated in 1978 during the war,
as well as for little Vimol and Tepvaddei,
who I hope will read this in school someday.
—SR

for Rachel
—J & MST

Text copyright © 1995 by Minfong Ho and Saphan Ros
Illustrations copyright © 1995 by Jean and Mou-sien Tseng
All rights reserved. No part of this book may be reproduced or utilized in any form or by any means, electronic or mechanical, including photocopying and recording, or by any information storage and retrieval system, without permission in writing from the Publisher. Inquiries should be addressed to Lothrop, Lee & Shepard Books, a division of William Morrow & Company, Inc., 1350 Avenue of the Americas, New York, New York 10019. Printed in the United States of America.
First Edition   1 2 3 4 5 6 7 8 9 10
Library of Congress Cataloging in Publication Data
Ho, Minfong. The two brothers / Minfong Ho and Saphan Ros; illustrated by Jean and Mou-sien Tseng.
p.   cm. Summary: Brought up in a Buddhist monastery, two brothers go out into the world to very different fates, armed with the advice of a wise abbot.
ISBN 0-688-12550-6. — ISBN 0-688-12551-4 (lib. bdg.) [1. Folklore—Cambodia.] I. Ros, Saphan.
II.Tseng, Jean, ill. III. Tseng, Mou-sien, ill. IV. Title. PZ8.1.H6674Tw 1994 [398.2'0959602—dc20 94-14516 CIP AC

IN A QUIET BUDDHIST MONASTERY IN CAMBODIA, there once lived two brothers named Kem and Sem. Orphaned when they were young, they grew up as close and as alike as two lotus seeds in a pod.

Both studied hard at the temple school, and eventually they were ordained as monks. For the next five years, they lived the simple, secluded life of monks, collecting the food offered them by villagers every morning, and sitting in quiet prayer every evening.

Then one day they went to the abbot of their monastery, knelt before him, and solemnly touched their heads to the ground.

"We have lived our entire lives in the monastery," they said. "Now we would like to see the world outside."

The abbot nodded. "You may go, and with my blessings," he told them. Then, in silence, he consulted his astrological charts.

He saw that the older brother, Kem, would become a very wealthy man, and to help fulfill the prophecy, he told Kem, "Go to China and become a merchant there."

As for the younger brother, the abbot saw that Sem would eventually become a king. But how? What advice should he give Sem so that the prophecy would come to pass?

The abbot looked at the younger brother's eager face and gave him the following advice: "When in love, look at the girl's mother. When in pain, don't sleep. And when in bed, don't talk. If you follow these words of advice, you will go far."

Bowing low before the abbot, the brothers thanked him and departed.

Kem decided to take the abbot's advice immediately. Bringing with him an ivory tusk and some jars of cardamom spice to trade, he boarded a ship bound for China.

Sem, uncertain what to do next, stayed on in the village nearby. There he fell in love with Bopha, a pretty village girl with a flashing smile. Bewitched by her charm, he completely forgot the abbot's words. Ignoring the fact that Bopha's mother was a shrewish old market woman who often cheated her customers, he married the girl.

Life was not easy for Sem and his pretty young wife. He could find no work other than odd jobs around the village, so they barely had enough to eat, and only ragged clothes to wear.

Tired and hungry as he often was, Sem still went down to the docks every few days to ask for any news of his brother. One day a large oceangoing Chinese junk sailed in, its square canvas sails flapping in the sea breeze. Sem waited until it had anchored and moored, then went on board.

"Tell me, do you know of a young Cambodian who is now living in China?" he asked.

"There *is* one Cambodian there," said the captain of the junk, "and he is the richest man in China."

Sem's heart skipped a beat. "When are you sailing back to China?" he asked.

"As soon as we load up on ivory and cardamom," the captain told him.

"Please, sir," Kem asked, "could I sail with you?"

When the captain gave his consent, Sem ran home and breathlessly told Bopha the news. "If that rich man in China is indeed my brother, I am sure he will help me when he sees how poor and miserable I am. Maybe I will come home a rich man myself. Be a good wife and wait at home for me."

His pretty wife just looked at him and smiled.

Three days later, Sem sailed off on the oceangoing junk. No sooner had he left than Bopha began to flirt with another man in the village.

Unaware of this, Sem reached China in high spirits. Before getting off the boat, he asked the captain, "When are you sailing back to Cambodia?"

"In three days," said the captain. "As soon as we load up on silk and tea leaves."

Eagerly Sem set off to look for his brother.

At the main gate of the biggest house in town, Sem asked the guard, "Is the master of this house a Cambodian named Kem?"

"Yes, he is," the guard answered. "But why do you ask? Where are you from?"

"I am from Cambodia," Sem told him, "and I am Kem's brother."

The guard stared at Sem's

ragged clothes, bare feet, and tousled hair. This man could not be his master's brother!

"Go on," Sem urged. "Announce to your master that his brother has arrived."

"My master is not in," said the guard.

"Tell his wife, then," Sem said.

Reluctantly the guard went into the courtyard of the big house and told his master's wife of the strange beggar from Cambodia waiting at the gate.

"Send him away," said the wife.

"He won't leave," said the guard.

"Then take him to the stables and chain him up," the wife snapped.

Finding himself chained and locked inside the dirty stables, Sem wept and wailed. "Have I come all this way to China to look for my long-lost brother, only to be imprisoned, maybe even killed, by him?"

When Kem came home, he heard Sem's voice weeping in the stables.

"Who is that weeping and wailing?" he asked his wife.

"Some mad beggar who claims to be your brother," she told him. "Why don't you just give the order to have him killed?"

Kem frowned. He did have a brother, after all. Unlikely as it seemed, suppose, just suppose, this was really Sem.

"Bring the beggar to me," he told the guard.

So the guard unchained Sem and brought him into the grand reception room.

The two brothers looked at each other, Kem plump and richly attired in a brocade gown, Sem lean and dusty in his torn sarong.

"Brother!" they called, and held out their hands to each other.

"Why are you so poor?" Kem asked Sem. "And what are you doing here?"

"I couldn't find much work at home," said Sem, "so I became poorer and poorer."

"How did you come here?"

"On a large oceangoing junk."

"When are you going back?"

"In three days," said Sem, "when the ship is fully laden with silk and tea leaves."

"That sounds like one of my ships," Kem said. Then he invited his brother to stay in his house.

Over dinner, they shared their memories of their simple childhood in the monastery, and of the abbot there.

"Why should your fortune be so good, when my life has been so miserable?" Sem wondered wistfully.

"Who knows?" said Kem. "Perhaps it is because I followed the abbot's advice, and you did not."

Sem took another sip of wine. He did not answer.

For three days, Sem stayed on at his brother's mansion, enjoying the fine food and wine. When it was time for him to return to the ship, Kem bade his brother farewell.

"Have a safe journey," said Kem. And as a parting gift, he gave Sem a single pair of new trousers and a bolt of cloth.

Is that all? Sem thought as he looked at these small gifts. His heart heavy with disappointment, he made his way down to the docks.

As the junk sailed off, Sem stood alone on the deck and watched the shoreline of China recede into the distance. Even after night fell, he remained there, staring into the darkness.

He thought back to the years when he had played in the temple courtyard with his brother. They were so alike then—why were their lives turning out so differently now?

The sea was still, and the sailors had all been lulled to sleep. Tired and sad, Sem settled down to sleep, too. But just then, the parting words of the abbot came back to him: "When in pain, don't sleep."

For the first time, Sem thought hard about the abbot and his advice. He remembered the old man's words, and he made a silent vow to live his life strictly in accordance with them from that moment on.

And so, while the others aboard the ship slept on, Sem remained awake.

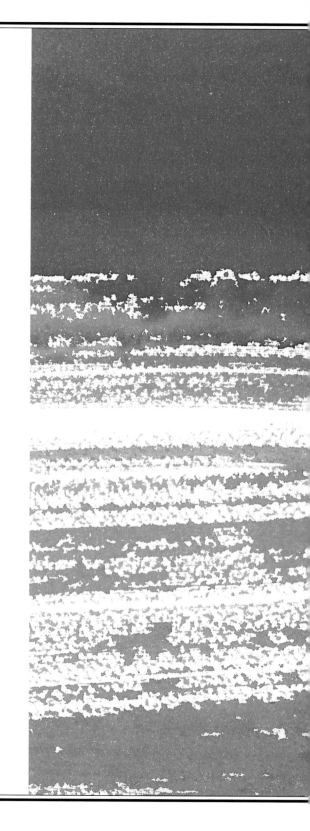

At midnight, Sem was the only one awake to hear a sudden rumbling from the sea. He turned around and saw a sea ogre whirling onto the junk. Just as the ogre was about to snatch a sleeping sailor, Sem sprang up, grasped the ogre's beard, and yanked it hard.

"Let go, or I will kill you with my bare hands!" Sem shouted.

Startled, the ogre tried to get away, but Sem held on so tightly that it was frightened. "Please, sir, release me," it begged, "and I will give you three wonderful treasures!"

"Give me the treasures first," said Sem.

The ogre dropped a stick, a rope, and a cooking pot onto the deck. "This magic stick will beat your enemies. This magic rope will tie them all up. And this magic pot will cook whatever you wish," the ogre said. "Now please let me go."

Sem let go of the ogre's beard, and away it went.

When Sem finally arrived back in his village, it was nighttime. His house was quiet, and his front door was locked. Knocking softly, he whispered, "Bopha, my love, open the door to me."

But Bopha was inside with her new boyfriend. So she pretended not to recognize Sem's voice. "Who's that calling me?" she asked. "My husband isn't home. Go away."

How faithful she is, Sem thought happily. "But I *am* your husband, dearest. Let me in."

"Sem, is it really you?" said Bopha. "Wait just a minute. Let me get a torch." Then she quickly let her boyfriend out the back window.

Meanwhile, Sem dug a hole beneath the house steps and hid his treasures there.

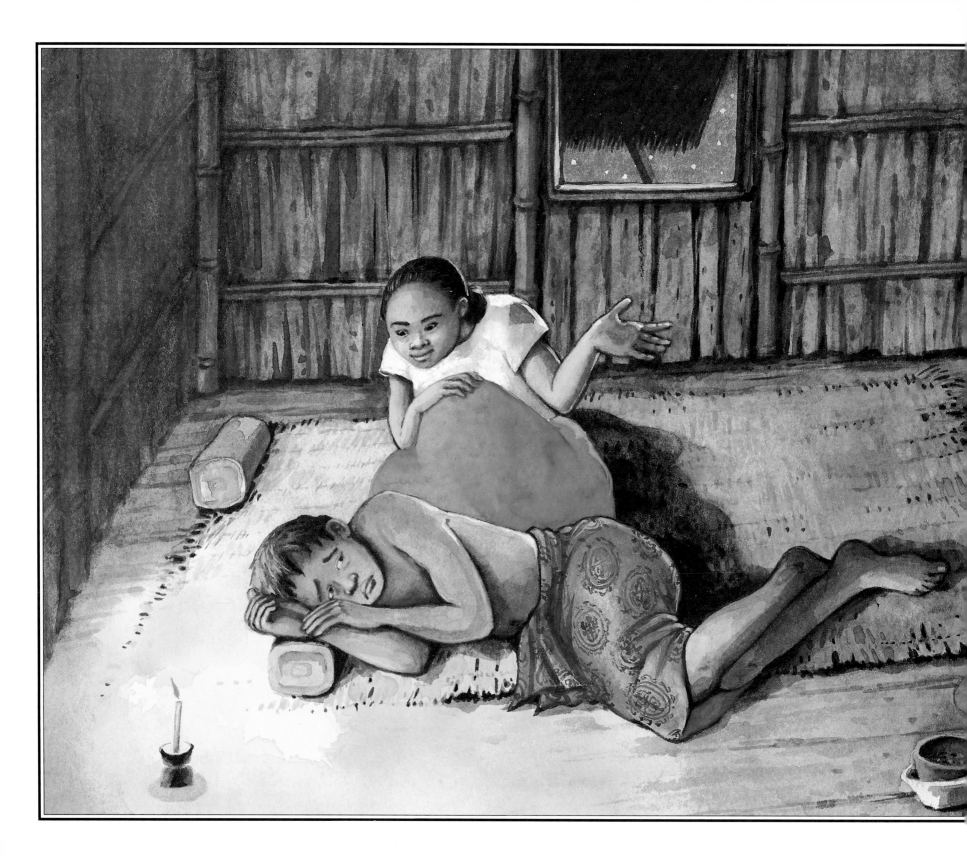

When the front door was finally opened, Bopha greeted him warmly. She prepared food for him, then led him to bed.

"And what did you bring me from China?" she asked as they settled down to sleep.

"My brother gave me a piece of cloth and a pair of pants," Sem told her.

"That can't be true!" Bopha cried. "You must have brought back something else!"

Sem remembered the words of the abbot: "When in bed, don't talk." So he remained silent.

"Come, tell me what else you've brought back," Bopha insisted.

"I'll tell you in the morning," Sem said.

But his wife kept questioning him, and finally Sem told her about the magic stick, the magic rope, and the magic cooking pot hidden beneath their front steps.

Now Bopha's new boyfriend was outside the window all this time, listening. And when he heard this, he crept beneath the steps, dug out the treasures, and ran off with them.

The next morning, when Sem discovered that his treasures were gone, he knew that Bopha had a secret boyfriend.

Grimly he dragged the house steps to the village court and demanded justice. "I hid my three treasures beneath these steps last night, and now they are gone," Sem announced. "I want to bring these steps to justice!"

The judges thought he was crazy. They laughed at him and told him to go away.

So Sem dragged his steps through the village until he reached the palace gates. There he made such a commotion that the King could not help but notice him. "What are you doing dragging those steps around?" he asked Sem. So Sem told him the whole story. The King nodded thoughtfully. "I understand your problem," he said, "and I have an idea." He handed Sem two beautiful gold silk sarongs. "Take these clothes home and give them to your wife. When you hear an announcement for a court play, don't go, but let *her* go. And make sure that she wears one of these sarongs."

Sem thanked the King and returned to his home.

When Bopha saw the beautiful clothes, she embraced Sem and pretended to love him more than ever.

The next day, the King's heralds beat their gongs through the village, spreading the news of a court play and inviting all the villagers to attend.

"Let's go see the play," Bopha said to Sem.

"No, I'm not going," Sem replied. "But you go ahead. And wear that new sarong of gold silk."

When she heard that, Bopha was thrilled. Secretly she gave the other sarong to her new boyfriend, and together they went to the play at the palace, each wearing clothes of gold silk.

But, unknown to them, the King had ordered his guards to arrest any couple who came to his play dressed in gold silk. So as soon as Bopha and her boyfriend entered the palace, they were caught and brought before the King.

Sem, too, was summoned to the court, where he stood facing the couple dressed in matching sarongs.

"Take a good look, Sem," said the King. "Is your wife here?"

"Yes, Your Majesty," Sem replied.

"Where is she?"

Sem pointed to Bopha.

"And what about the man next to her? Do you know him?"

"No, Your Majesty, I do not."

"Well, I do," said the King. He turned to the man dressed in gold. "You are the one who stole Sem's wife. Is that not so?"

"Yes," the man admitted.

"And what's more, you are the one who stole the treasures from beneath Sem's steps. Is that not true?"

Seeing that the King already knew everything, the man could only say "Yes" again.

The King then ordered the thief to return everything he had stolen from Sem.

When the magic stick, the magic rope, and the magic pot were brought into the court, the King faced the couple in gold sarongs and declared that they would both have to be punished. "Stick, stick, beat the thief!" he commanded.

Immediately the magic stick flew into the air and hit the thief so hard that he cried out in pain.

"Rope, rope, bind the wife!" the King commanded.

Immediately the rope twisted itself around Bopha and tied her up securely.

The magic stick might still be beating the thief, and the magic rope still binding Bopha, had it not been for the Queen, who now stepped forward and placed a gentle hand on the King's arm.

"These two have been punished enough," she said. "There is no need to be so bitter." She picked up the magic pot. "Pot, pot, cook us a nice sweet bean porridge!" she commanded.

When the pot had filled itself with a fragrant sweet porridge, the Queen passed it around. And as soon as the King had tasted its sweetness, he decided to call off the magic stick and rope.

"You are both forgiven," he told the couple in gold. Then he looked straight at Bopha. "From this day on, you are no longer married to Sem. Go with your thief, and never return."

Their heads lowered in shame, the couple then left the court.

"As for you, Sem," the King continued, "here are your three treasures. You may take them all back now."

Sem bowed low. "Thank you, sire, but they are yours," he said, "in gratitude for your help. The magic stick will fight all your enemies, the magic rope will tie them up, and the magic pot will cook any delicacy you wish."

Speechless with surprise, the King did not know how to thank Sem for these precious gifts. But the Queen smiled. "Your gifts are truly wonderful," she said. "We will treasure them as we treasure our only child." And so saying, she presented her daughter, the shy young princess, to Sem.

Sem took one look at the graceful princess and fell in love. But this time he remembered the words of the abbot: "When in love, look at the girl's mother." He saw that the Queen was not only beautiful but wise and kind, and he realized that her daughter would be, as well.

Sem gazed mutely at the princess, wanting to ask for her hand in marriage, but not daring to.

The Queen smiled. "Yes, you may marry her," she told Sem.

A few weeks hence, a grand wedding was held in the palace. Sem's brother, Kem, sailed in from China in a ship laden with enough silk and tea leaves for all the wedding guests, and there was feasting all day and dancing under the full moon all night.

Eventually, many, many full moons later, the old King died. And so it came about that Sem became King of all Cambodia, just as the abbot in his quiet monastery had foreseen.